Rainbow
Reading Rainboom!

By Tallulah May
Illustrated by Zoe Persico

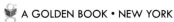 A GOLDEN BOOK • NEW YORK

Licensed by:

HASBRO and its logo, MY LITTLE PONY, and all related characters are trademarks of Hasbro
and are used with permission.
© 2018 Hasbro. All Rights Reserved.

Published in the United States by Golden Books, an imprint of Random House Children's Books,
a division of Penguin Random House LLC, 1745 Broadway, New York, NY 10019, and in Canada by
Penguin Random House Canada Limited, Toronto. Golden Books, A Golden Book, A Little Golden Book,
the G colophon, and the distinctive gold spine are registered trademarks of Penguin Random House LLC.

rhcbooks.com

ISBN 978-0-525-57789-8 (trade) – ISBN 978-0-525-57790-4 (ebook)

Printed in the United States of America

10 9 8 7 6 5 4 3 2 1

Rainbow Dash is so excited to get her books signed by her favorite author, A. K. Yearling!

While standing in line with Twilight Sparkle, she sees a familiar face. It's her old Junior Speedster Flight Camp instructor, Puddle Jump! He's a fan, too.

Puddle Jump explains that even though he **loves books**, he can't convince his students to get excited about reading.

"Maybe you both could come and mentor our fillies. I know they'd love to hear from a great flier like you, Rainbow Dash!" Puddle Jump says.

Well, I **am** kind of **awesome**, so . . . sure!

The next day, Twilight and Rainbow Dash show up at Flight Camp. Twilight brings her favorite books of spells and history, while Rainbow Dash brings everything A. K. Yearling has ever written.

A huge group of fillies swarms them
the moment they arrive. Everypony wants
Rainbow Dash's autograph.

Thankfully, Puddle Jump arrives and gets his students to settle down. He explains that Rainbow Dash and Twilight Sparkle are going to be their mentors for the day.

"Is Rainbow Dash going to show us how to make a **Sonic Rainboom**?" one filly interrupts.

"Or tell us about that time she flew through **Ghastly Gorge**?" yells another.

"Can she tell us what the **Wonderbolts** are really like?" begs a third.

Rainbow is swept up in all the excitement. She starts to tell the students about her favorite flying moments, but Twilight gently interrupts. **"Actually,"** she explains, "we're here to help you with reading!"

The class **greans.** But Rainbow Dash isn't
worried. She's going to read to them from her
favorite **Daring Do** books. Surely A. K. Yearling
will get them **excited about READING!**

Rainbow Dash is so wrapped up in the story that she doesn't notice the entire class is asleep until she hears a big SNOOOOOOOOOOORE.

"**what?** But . . . but how can they **not** like Daring Do?" she cries.

Twilight Sparkle suggests that it might be time to take a break.

"Everypony learns a little differently," says Twilight. "Don't worry. We'll find a way to get through to them."

Minutes later, the fillies are up and outside practicing drills.

"Let's try the **Cumbersome Quadrilateral formation**," one filly pipes up. "Commander Easyglider invented it himself in the fourth celestial era."

Another filly wants to try something a bit more complicated.

A third wants to see if they can fly even faster.
"Maybe if we fold our wings in closer, we'll be
able to reduce the air friction and go as fast as
Rainbow Dash!"

Tired after their long afternoon with the fillies, Rainbow Dash sits next to Twilight, whose nose is deep in her history book.

"I'm looking up that move you guys tried earlier, and it's actually even older than we thought. It dates back to the **first** celestial era!" Twilight says.

Instead of answering, Rainbow Dash grabs Twilight's book and zooms away with it!

"Hey!" says Twilight, shocked. "It's not **that** boring."

In the air, Rainbow calls to the filly leading the flight drills. "You know the Cumbersome Quadrilateral? It's actually **older** than we thought!

"And there are more historical flight patterns in this book. **Look!** It's the **Flying Cobra**—which comes from the Crystal Kingdom," Rainbow Dash explains. The fillies are fascinated.

THE FLYINGCOBRA

EST 1212-0

1. GAIN MOMENTUM

2. PREPARE FOR ANGULAR UPWARD TURN

3. mesh

Twilight Sparkle suddenly realizes what
Rainbow Dash is doing and jumps right in to help.
"This art book has all sorts of different
cloud-sculpture designs you can try!" she says.

"You should check out this chapter about aerodynamics!" Rainbow Dash says.

Soon they've given away lots of books to the students.

"Wow! I can't believe you got all the fillies to be interested in reading," Puddle Jump observes. "Who knew reading could be so cool!" a filly shouts.

And all the other fillies agree!